December, 2006

Dear Dad,

I bought this ___ ___
read it and feel it ___
sentiment about the relationship
you have with your grandchildren.
I know the littlest ones often
overwhelm and frazzle you but in
spite of that, you are always
there.

Thank you so much for providing
a wonderful place for Caleb and
Nia while I was in the hospital.

I am so grateful that you
provided such a wonderful example
of a righteous priesthood holder while
we were growing up. I truly
believe it inspired your daughters to
strive for that in their own marriages
and homes.

Thank you! You're awesome! I'll love
you forever!!! Your Daughter,
Caralyn

For Grandpas Stan, Stanley,
Irv, Fred, and Richard
—H.M.Z.

Text copyright © 2006 by Harriet Ziefert
Illustrations copyright © 2006 by Deborah Zemke
All rights reserved
CIP Data is available.
Published in the United States 2006 by
Blue Apple Books
515 Valley Street, Maplewood, N.J. 07040
www.blueapplebooks.com
Distributed in the U.S. by Chronicle Books

First Edition
Printed in China

ISBN 13: 978-1-59354-097-5
ISBN 10: 1-59354-097-3

1 3 5 7 9 10 8 6 4 2

That's What Grandpas Are For

Harriet Ziefert

pictures by Deborah Zemke

BLUE APPLE BOOKS

GRANDPA

If we are late and miss the bus . . .

Grandpa will drive us to school—
even if he hasn't shaved yet.

That's what grandpas are for.

If we go fishing, and I don't
want to put the bait on the hook,

Grandpa will do it for me.

That's what grandpas are for.

If I climb to the top of
the tallest tree in the yard
and then find out that up
is easy, but down is hard . . .

Grandpa will rescue me.

If I am dressed in jeans and
an old shirt and Daddy wants me to
put on clean clothes, or stay home,

Grandpa will say I look fine
and take me out to lunch anyway.

That's what grandpas are for.

If I forget the difference
between a stalactite and a stalagmite,
Grandpa will remind me,
"Stalactites from the ceiling grow,
   Stalagmites from the ground below."

If I am unhappy and I tell Grandpa
I want to run away to Australia,
he will offer to go with me.

That's what grandpas are for.

If it's my birthday,
Grandpa will do a magic trick
and pull a silver dollar out of my ear.

If I am scared and can't fall asleep, Grandpa will tell me a story about his first day of school a gazillion years ago and how he was so frightened he hid under his desk.

He will not say, "Boys your age should be able to go to sleep by themselves."

Grandpa says I'm pretty even
when my hair's not brushed and
I have a chocolate milk mustache.

Grandpa holds my hand
even when it's dirty.

Grandpa lets us stay up late.

That's what grandpas are for!

grandchildren

If I feel like singing old songs,
my grandchildren sing with me.

That's what grandchildren are for.

When I read the newspaper,
my grandson brings me
tea and cookies.

If I think that I have learned pretty
much everything worth knowing,
I listen to my grandchildren
and learn that I am wrong.

That's what grandchildren are for.

If I quote Shakespeare, my
granddaughter doesn't groan
but says she wants to learn
Shakespeare, too.

If I am working hard to build a wall of rocks, my granddaughter helps—even though she doesn't really like to get her clothes dirty.

If I am weeding the garden, my grandson
pulls out the dandelions.

That's what grandchildren are for.

If I want to swim across the pond,
my grandson will be my buddy.

My granddaughter lets me come to her class play
and sit in the front row and take pictures.

And after the performance she proudly introduces me to her friends.

If I am alone and grumpy, my grandchildren can make me feel better.

That's what grandchildren are for.

My grandchildren make
every outing an adventure.

My granddaughter loves me when I'm grouchy and not just when I'm nice.

My grandson loves me when I make
a mistake and not just when I'm right.

If I don't have
much to do,

my grandchildren
keep me busy.

If my arms are empty, my
grandchildren fill them.

That's what grandchildren are for!